TEN IN A BED

TEN IN A BED

— Mary Rees —

Andersen Press·London

To Mum, Dad, Alastair and Vivien,
not forgetting Boxer and Sid

Copyright © 1988 by Mary Rees.
This special paperback edition first published in 2003 by Andersen Press Ltd.
The rights of Mary Rees to be identified as the author and illustrator of this work
have been asserted by her in accordance with the Copyright, Designs and Patents Act, 1988.
First published in Great Britain in 1988 by Andersen Press Ltd. 20 Vauxhall Bridge Road, London SW1V 2SA.
Published in Australia by Random House Australia Pty., 20 Alfred Street, Milsons Point, Sydney, NSW 2061.
All rights reserved. Colour separated in Switzerland by Photolitho AG, Zürich.
Printed and bound in China.

10 9 8 7 6 5 4 3 2 1

British Library Cataloguing in Publication Data available.

ISBN 1 84270 256 4

This book has been printed on acid-free paper

There were TEN in the bed
And the little one said,
"Roll over! Roll over!"
So they all rolled over
And one fell out . . .

There were NINE in the bed
And the little one said,
"Roll over! Roll over!"
So they all rolled over
And one fell out . . .

There were EIGHT in the bed
And the little one said,
"Roll over! Roll over!"
So they all rolled over
And one fell out . . .

There were SEVEN in the bed
And the little one said,
"Roll over! Roll over!"
So they all rolled over
And one fell out . . .

There were SIX in the bed
And the little one said,
"Roll over! Roll over!"
So they all rolled over
And one fell out . . .

There were FIVE in the bed
And the little one said,
"Roll over! Roll over!"
So they all rolled over
And one fell out . . .

There were FOUR in the bed
And the little one said,
"Roll over! Roll over!"
So they all rolled over
And one fell out . . .

There were THREE in the bed
And the little one said,
"Roll over! Roll over!"
So they all rolled over
And one fell out . . .

There were TWO in the bed
And the little one said,
"Roll over! Roll over!"
So they all rolled over
And one fell out . . .

There was ONE in the bed
And the little one said,
"I'm not getting up!"
The other NINE said,
"Oh yes you are!"

Then there were NONE in the bed
And no one said,
"Roll over! Roll over!"